Stop Kissing Me, Mommy!

Nadine Chevolleau

Library and Archives Canada Cataloguing in Publication

Chevolleau, Nadine, 1970-, author
        Stop Kissing Me, Mommy! / Nadine Chevolleau.

ISBN 978-0-9919525-0-2 (pbk.)

        I. Title.

PS8605.H487S76 2013   jC813'.6   C2013-902599-5

First published by Nadine Chevolleau in 2013.

About the Author:

Nadine Chevolleau lives in Toronto, Canada with her husband, and three boys.
She currently works as a marketing professional in the media industry.
She's happy to report that her kiss-oholic ways are now under control
(most of the time), and that she and Bryce have an agreement that morning
and bed-time kisses are a-okay.

Stop Kissing Me, Mommy! is her first book. She's currently working on another
children's book and a cookbook, which will be published in 2014.
www.stopkissingmemommy.com

Dedicated to: Papa Dada Guy – DCTW, Bryce, Joshua, Jordan

Special thanks to a very talented illustrator, Georgia Stylou and editor, Ann Westlake.

When I was a very little baby my mommy loved to kiss me.

She kissed my forehead,

my cheeks, my lips and my nose.

She even kissed my fingers and my toes.

It was a lot of kisses.

And I liked it.

When I was a **bigger** baby my mommy was still
big on this **kissing thing.**
She loved **to kiss** my forehead, my cheeks, my lips and my nose.
And, yup, she **still kissed** my fingers and my toes.

It was a lot of **kisses**.

And I liked it - most of the time.

However, when I turned two years old, this whole **kissing thing** was starting to get **on my nerves.**
I mean gosh, how many times does she have **to kiss me?**

I wake up in **the morning** and
there she is leaning in for **a kiss.**
That's cool.
I understand the whole **morning kiss** thing.

But then she changes my diaper
and gives me **another kiss.**
For what?
Changing my smelly diaper!

Do you understand **what I mean?**

I eat **breakfast** and Mommy gives me **another kiss**, and washes my face – another kiss!

Grandma's Porridge

The day I turned three I made **an important** decision.

Now that I could sort of

put a sentence together

I decided to tell my mommy **to stop kissing me!**

The next **morning,** my mommy came into **my room.**
As usual, she leaned in
for a big, fat,
juicy kiss.

I took a **deep** breath and,
at the top of my lungs, I hollered

"STOP KISSING ME, MOMMY!"

She leaned back,
with a **look** of surprise on her face.
Hmmm, I thought, that will **STOP** her.

She looked at me, and said with a grin,
"Bryce, I'll never stop kissing you."

Then Mommy scooped me up in her arms
and kissed my whole face!

It tickled **so much** that
I started laughing
and laughing...
but I wasn't **happy** about it.

The **next day** I tried again,

using my loudest **voice** ever.

"Stop kissing me, Mommy!"

My mommy **smiled** at me and said,

"Bryce, I'll **never** stop kissing you."

Then she scooped me up in her arms and

kissed my **whole face**! I didn't

want **to laugh,** but I just couldn't help it.

The next morning Mommy walked into my room.

There was something different about her.

I took a **deep** breath and started to shout, **"Stop kissing..."** but before I could finish, she picked me **up** and gave me **a hug**, but no kiss.

Wow! I thought, I think she finally got the message.

In fact, Mommy **didn't give me**
any **kisses** the whole day.

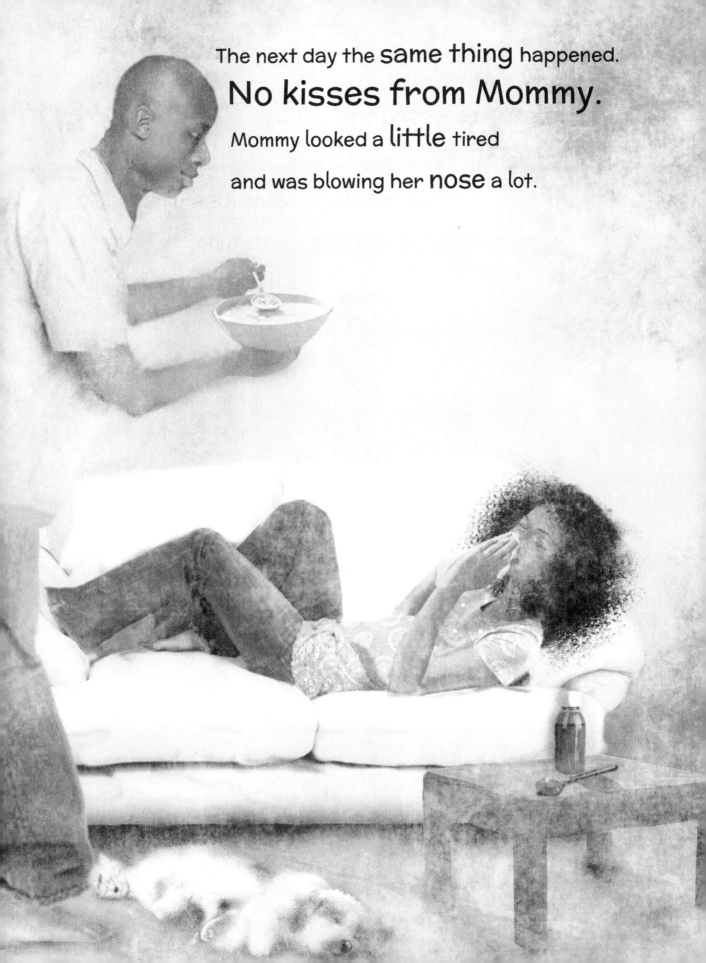

The next day the **same thing** happened.
No kisses from Mommy.
Mommy looked a **little** tired

and was blowing her **nose** a lot.

Something **strange**

started happening to me too.

At the end of my second **kiss-free day**,

my heart started to feel a little funny;

a **little** achy breaky.

I don't know why...

Could it be...

I missed my mommy's kisses?

The next **morning**

my mommy came into my room.

She **didn't look** tired anymore

and she had her

usual **happy voice** back.

I heard her tell Daddy that her cold was **all gone**.

Mommy came over to my bed and **before** she knew it, I reached **up**, wrapped my arms around her **tightly** and gave HER a big, fat, juicy **kiss**.

"Mommy," I said, "I'll **never** stop **kissing** you!"

CPSIA information can be obtained at www.ICGtesting.com
Printed in the USA
LVOW02s1736251013

358654LV00001B/1/P